Overturned Hearts: A Shakespearean Tale

By Margherita Smith

ISBN: 978-0-9961966-0-4

ELIZABETHAN TIMES

This is the tale of Anne Cecil, the daughter of Queen Elizabeth's chief counselor, Lord Burghley. It tells of the ups and downs of her relationship to one of the era's highest ranking nobles, Lord Oxford.

The setting is the sixteenth century, a time very different from ours.

Coffee and tea had not yet come to England, and river water was dirty, so everyone drank ale or beer, wine or mead, and was probably in some degree inebriated most of their waking hours. It was a tipsy time.

Baths were considered unhealthy; most people bathed maybe twice a year; water closets had not taken the place of privies; the contents of chamber pots were tossed out of windows; and the horses in the streets did not use chamber pots. The River Thames was an open sewer. It was a malodorous time.

Bear-baiting, bull-baiting, dog fighting and cock fighting were popular sports. Torture was officially condoned. Executions were public entertainment. Convicted criminals were hanged and left to rot on the gallows or cut down and drawn and quartered while still breathing. Nobles were allowed the mercy of beheading, but then their heads were mounted on pikes at the gate to London Bridge and left to the birds and the worms. It was a cruel, gruesome time.

Still, it was a time of deep religious spirit, of fervent Christianity, of frequent prayers, pious books, sermons, and services—and great controversy between

Catholicism and Protestantism. Under Bloody Mary, more than 300 Protestants were burned at the stake (to save their souls). Under Queen Elizabeth, Catholic leaders, including Mary, Queen of Scots, were beheaded (to save Elizabeth's throne). Church and state were *not* separate. In fact, for some of the main characters in this story, it was a time of servin g God by serving his regent, Queen Elizabeth.

She was called Glories and Georgiana for good reason: under her aegis, Drake circumnavigated the globe; England defeated the Spanish Armada; and the East India Company was founded. It was a time of vigor and achievement.

And it was a time of immense literary grace—from William Shakespeare, John Lyly, Thomas Kyd, Christopher Marlowe, Ben Johnson, George Peele, Thomas Nashe, George Chapman, Philip Sidney, Francis Bacon, Edmund Spenser, Charles Lamb, Sir Walter Raleigh, and many other inspired writers—and a bit later, the King James Bible.

When the story of Anne Cecil begins, her father was a knight, not a peer. He was Sir William Cecil, not yet Lord Burghley (the queen made him a baron later). Even so, as the Queen Elizabeth's chief counselor, he was one of the most powerful men in England.

This is a love story from the days when marriage for love among the gentry and nobility was uncommon. But it's a love story with a history that contemporaries of the principals cited as an example of why marriage for love is inadvisable.

Anne Cecil met Edward DeVere, Lord Oxford, when she was six years old, and he was twelve. Here is how it came about.

"What was all the flurry I heard last evening?" she asked when her nurse woke her.

"A visitor," Nurse Emily answered, "A surprise. I am to take you to meet him in your father's library as soon as you dress and break your fast."

Sir William Cecil's library, one of the greatest in Europe, was housed in a large bright room with three walls covered with shelf after shelf of books and papers. Extending on each side of the single window on the fourth wall was a long table with half a dozen chairs drawn up to it.

When Anne entered, Cecil and the twelve-year-old Lord Oxford were standing by the table. She ran to her father's tall, lean, broad-shouldered figure and raised her arms for him to lift her up.

"Good morrow, dear Papa, sir, I trust you are well and not burdened by all these books and papers," she said in his arms, and kissed his long, narrow nose.

"Good morrow, Tannakin, my sweeting, I am well and thou art saucy as usual," he answered, and twirled her around before he put her down at Nurse Emily's side.

"My lord," he said to the sturdy, self-possessed boy standing next to him, "may I present my daughter, Miss Anne Mildred Cecil."

What the boy saw was a slender little girl with a lively, cheerful face, brown hair under a lace cap, a mouth perpetually curved upwards, and alert brown eyes.

The boy nodded to her.

"Anne," said her father, "may I present to thee Edward DeVere, Viscount Bulbeck, the Earl of Oxford. Her Majesty hath commanded me to bring him to live with us for a time as my ward."

I like his looks, Anne thought when she looked at the boy's candid blue eyes and arched brows in a face framed with blonde curls and the hairline that we now call a widow's peak.

Anne nodded.

Nurse Emily sniffed in reproof.

"Curtsey," whispered Nurse Emily.

"Must I curtsey, sir?" whispered Anne to her father. "He is naught but a boy!"

"Curtsey!" commanded her father quietly. "He is the seventeenth Earl of Oxford, which is a title amongst the oldest in the realm, a title of consequence."

Anne curtseyed so low that she swayed, and her nurse had to help her keep her balance. She stifled a laugh and curtseyed again with grace and composure.

"I do beg pardon, my lord," she said to the boy, "I knew not that an earl might be so young. Those I have met heretofore are as venerable as my father. But, my lord, I now see you have the presence of a peer."

He smiled and bowed deeply.

"Thy apology is nearly as pretty as thy face," he said. "And if thou art as lovely when full grown, I will marry thee and make thee a countess."

"Oh," said Anne, and curtseyed again, "And you do that, my lord, I will have to love, honor, and keep you, in sickness and in health all your life."

"He is jesting, Anne," said Cecil, "My lord, it befits you not to make such a frivolous promise."

"Indeed, venerable sir," said Oxford, "I will take good care to be befitting hereafter."

Anne giggled. *'Venerable,' as I had called him,* she thought, *and 'befitting.' He is impudent and charming, and I like him already, but I don't think I want to be a countess. Papa has often told me to be proud of who I am.*

(Who she was, of course, was the daughter of the senior advisor to the queen, a knight who had taught her to respect but not to envy those of higher rank.)

Oxford caught his breath at Anne's giggle. All through his dozen years, he had been treated with somber deference. No one had laughed at his mild jokes; no one had recognized them as jokes. He smiled at Anne in appreciation.

"Thou hast a fine sense of the jocund and the jovial," he said, pleased to display his ready vocabulary.

At this point in the story, I will cease using most of the *thees* and *thous* that were standard in those times to address friends, children, servants, and social inferiors. Just assume that the Elizabethan dialogue hereafter has been translated into current usage, albeit with an Elizabethan flavor.

"My lord," said Cecil, "I would have you know the reason I have brought you together with my daughter this morning."

"I have heard that you are a superior scholar despite your youth, and I have hired the finest of tutors for you—Laurence Nowell and Sir Thomas Smith. However, they will not arrive for several weeks. In the meantime, we must address other concerns—your bodily health, for one, for I have heard that you have neglected athletics and have preferred study to games and reading to sport."

"It was not my doing, Sir William. My father saw to it that I am a fair horseman and not a bad bowman. But he was not often home, and my only friends were books."

"And books can be good friends. But a lively mind requires a strong body, and riding and archery are not comprehensive exercise. Now, a further concern is your character, for I have also heard that you have become willful and unruly."

"I protest, sir."

"Good. In such a cause, protest is good. Mayhap it will reveal to you that learning must go hand in hand with wisdom, especially amongst those born to privilege. Therefore, my lord, I have contrived to fill your days with worthy ventures. In the evenings, your uncle, Arthur Golding, who as you know is living here whilst translating Ovid's *Metamorphoses*, will spend an hour tutoring you in biblical studies."

"My father could not suffer what he called Uncle Arthur's 'upright righteousness,' but I like him, and here he has already presented me with a Bible, sir," said Oxford, "and assigned me the book of Philippians to read and mark where a passage strikes me, he says, begin to find true religion, true godliness, and true virtue."

"Splendid," Cecil responded. "The assignment aims true towards a desirable result. So, preceding your evening exercise in finding—what was it?—your true religion, true godliness, and true virtue—in the afternoons you will exercise your body and your sense of fair play in sports and athletics under the tutelage of my son Thomas."

Oxford clapped his hands. "That will be no chore, sir," he said. "I'm very strong and agile. I hope there will be wrestling."

"No wrestling. No violence except for fencing. You must practice peaceful alternatives, my lord. To that end, before the afternoon's activity, in the mornings you will exercise your patience and indulgence for others by teaching Anne how to read and write."

"Sir . . ." said Anne.

"Hush, child. I will endure no opposition. The lessons have been delayed long enough."

"But . . ."

"Did you hear me?" he said sharply.

"Aye, sir, I will button up my mouth," she said, and twisted her lips with her hand.

"I know that your mother does not approve of these lessons, Tannakin. I have overruled her. Instead of spinning and the other ladylike activities your mother assigns you daily, for the next few weeks in the mornings you will come here to the library to study with Lord Oxford."

The boy smiled. "I promise, Mistress Anne, that you will read and write nothing unladylike. And I promise to be a patient and indulgent teacher. We shall both enjoy the lessons," he said.

Cecil continued. "Here on the table, my lord, is the equipment you will need."

And he named each item as he picked it up. "Wax tablets, stylus, quills, penknife, inkpot, sand shaker, hornbook, Aesop's Fables, and some other books, including my newest acquisition from Switzerland, the Bible of the Church of Geneva."

"Nurse Emily will stay here with Anne, and when it is time, the two of them will show you the way to the high table in the great hall for dinner at noon. There you will meet my son Thomas whom you will accompany this afternoon. Good day to you then, My Lord. I go to the palace. God go with you. We shall meet again at supper."

He bowed to Oxford, and pinched Anne's cheek, telling her, "Tannakin, behave yourself," and started to leave

"I forget how," Anne said mischievously.

Cecil turned around, picked her up, and set her on the table.

"What I plan to do," he said, "is tickle you until you recall how to behave yourself. Shall I begin?"

"Nay, nay, please, Papa, sir" she laughed. "My memory has returned. I will behave perfectly."

"Good girl," he said, lifted her down, patted her head, and said, "Farewell then. Just remember who you are and be true to yourself and your heritage."

He and Oxford exchanged bows, and he left the room. Anne and Oxford said their farewells; Oxford bowed to Anne; Anne curtsied to him, took Emily's hand, and the two left Oxford to acquaint himself with the library.

THE ABCs

At the first lesson with teacher Oxford, "My Lord," said Anne. "I tried to explain to my Papa that already I know how to read."

"Indeed? Why does he not know this?'

"I kept it a secret because of my mother, My Lord. Her father, my grandfather, Sir Anthony Cooke, was tutor to King Edward, and he brought her up to be a scholar. But her days are now filled with housewifery, and she believes that girls are better off without a scholarly bent, and that they must learn how to manage a household before they learn how to read and write."

"Who then taught you to read?"

"Oh, lud, I had no teacher. I sat on my mother's knee and followed the lines on the page when she read from King Edward's Book of Common Prayer every morning and every evening, and somehow I caught the knack."

"Truly? I thought I was the only one in the world with such a gift. When did you discover this, little one?"

"Not long ago. I haven't had much practice."

"I was younger than you—four, I think, when my father taught me the letters and I was soon able to realize I could see them together in words. But no matter, mayhap the talent is more burden than blessing. Well, you must show me how you do. Let us sit here at the table and go to work."

Oxford placed the hornbook before Anne. "Read this," he said.

Aa Bb Cc Dd Ee Ff Gg
Hh Ii Jj Kk Ll Mm Nn

Oo Pp Qq Rr Ss Tt Uu
Vv Ww Xx Yy Zz
& a e i o
oure father which arte in heven
halowed be thy name.
Let thy kyngdome come.
Thy wyll be fulfilled
as well in erth as it ys in heven.
Geve vs this daye oure dayly breede. And
forgeve vs oure oure treaspases
eve as we forgeve oure trespacers.
And leade vs not into teptacion:
but delyver vs fro evell.
For thyne is ye kyngedome
and ye power and ye glorye
for ever. Amen.
　　　　—Hornbook Lord's Prayer

"Here below on the hornbook," Anne said, "is the Our Father. I can read all the words very well, although of course I know it by heart. But up above I think are letters, and I do not know their names."

"It is the alphabet. Do you not know the alphabet? You read but you do not know the letters?"

She nodded. "Aye, I read, Nay, I don't know the alphabet," she said. She moved her head up and down and then from side to side. "Aye, nay, both," she said, giggling.

Oxford frowned. He had never witnessed such playfulness.

"It's a problem that is not humorous;" he said, "It is entirely serious. You need to learn the alphabet. I will teach you when we meet tomorrow."

On the morrow, after appropriate greetings, he put the hornbook on the table in front of her and began the lesson.

"Attend!" he said, and pointed to the letters on the hornbook as he named them, speaking with measured solemnity.

"Here is great A *per se* A, small a *per se* a, great B *per se* B, small b *per se* b, great C *per se* C . . ."

"Hold, my lord, I think I see how exceeding serious this is."

With the fingers of each hand Anne pulled down the corners of her mouth and spoke in imitation of his tone.

"The alphabet is the ABC," she said. "The alphabet, my lord, is the letters that make the words."

She stopped the imitation, "Oh, my lord, I did not know that, but I do know the ABC rhyme. I do know the names of the letters in the alphabet; my nurse taught them to me. I thought it was just nonsense verse:"

She smiled at Nurse Emily, who was standing in the nearest corner.

"You can read, Nurse?" asked Oxford. .

"Nay, your lordship," said Emily. "I too thought it was a children's nonsense verse."

"I am happy to know what an alphabet is,'" said Anne. She pulled the corners of her mouth up with her fingers and recited the rhyme brightly:

> A B C D E F G,
> H I J K L M N O P
> Q R S and T U V
> W X Y and Zed.
> And now I've said
> my ABCs
> I ask that you
> reward me, please.

She put her hands in her lap and frowned as she became earnest.

Thoughtfully and deliberately she pointed to the letters and read A "Great A *per se* A, small a *per se* A—they are the papa and the baby but they really don't look a bit alike; great B *per se* B, small b *per se* B—the papa has a hat on; great C *per se* C—and the papa's small son looks exactly like him, my lord."

"Enough," said Oxford, "you make me dizzy. Keep your comments to yourself, please. Just name the letters."

"Certainly, my lord," said Anne and went on to the end of the alphabet. "I like the dots over the J and the I. Is there a name for them?"

"I think they are just dots," he said.

"They deserve their own name. I shall call them jits," she said.

"You can't just invent words, Anne."

"Oh, dear, what a sad thing." Her face became distressed. "I could cry."

"Don't cry, Anne. I take it back. Not anyone can invent words, but you can. That dot is a jit."

"Oh, good. And another thing. I see that great I nod X and V are letters papa writes when he makes notes. He makes rows of them. What is he spelling?"

"He's doing sums, not spelling words. Those letters are numbers in Roman numerals. I'll teach you about them later. First we'll learn a new system, Arabic numerals."

"All right, teacher, but I think I won't like Arab numbers as well as Rome's.

""We'll see. Now back to work," he said, and pointed to the letters, in the hornbook. "Great I *per se* I, small i *per se* i with a jit. Great *J per se* J, small j *per se* j with a jit."

"And now," he asked, pointing to the symbol after the zed, "What is this?"

"It is 'and'," she said. "And *per se* and."

"And it has a name," he said, "ampersand." Her face brightened, her lips rounded, and her blue eyes widened with the pleasure of discovery. She hugged the hornbook to her.

"I love the alphabet," she said. "I love reading."

She is the prettiest girl I have ever seen, he thought. *And she is a darling.*

"Well," he said, taking the hornbook from her, "Aye, well, you are *well* on your way to becoming entirely familiar with the letters. Now you must learn to spell the words, for the first step towards writing is spelling."

"I will love spelling. I will love writing," she said.

"What you do now is this," he told her. "Speak the letters in every word here in the Paternoster. Say the word, then the letters, and then the word again, like this:

"Our, O, U, R, E, our. Father," she read, and slowly spelled it out, "F A T H E R."

She spelled her way through the lines of the prayer, more and more aptly as she went along. When she reached Forgive us, he stopped her and set her to writing the majuscule letters of the alphabet in block form.

"I think you do not need to start with a wax tablet," he said. "I think you are old enough to write with pen and ink. I will sharpen the quill when that is needed. What you must do is copy the skeleton form of the great letters one by one."

She set to work. As the morning came to an end, with a little help from Vere, she could write the block letter ABCs legibly.

"Time for your examination," Oxford said. "I shall devise an echo poem. Copy this as I both write it and speak it:

WHO READS AS WELL
AS ANY MAN?
ANNE.

She copied the lines and then continued writing her face intent, her teeth biting her lower lip. When she handed him the paper, he read aloud the new lines:

WHO YS A TECHER
WE RE VERE?
EDWERD DE VERE..

Nurse Emily applauded softly.

Oxford nodded at Emily approvingly and turned to Anne.

"You are a marvel, child," he said, as he crossed through the errors and wrote corrections, changing TECHER to TEACHER, EDWERD to EDWARD, and REVER*E* and DEVERE to single words.

She is clever indeed, he thought. *When she grows up I may well make her my countess.*

"Tomorrow I will begin to teach you the italic script," he said. "Then we can read and write every morning. Will that suit you?"

"Aye, oh, yes. I love being a student, my lord. I love being *your* student, my lord."

I do believe, he thought, *I will love being her teacher.*

"Vere," he said. "Call me Vere; it is one of my names, and I like it. When we are together here in the library, you will be Anne and I will be Vere. We will read to each other and practice writing."

"I like the name too, Vere, "she said, "I like it that Vere is here this year."

"And for nine more years till I reach my majority," said Vere.

(Here I, the writer, too, have begun calling him Vere. Others, depending on their relationship to him, will use Edward, Oxford, Lord Oxford, My Lord, or Your Lordship.)

Vere knew well how to exercise his intellect and his rank. But Anne's vivacity, her declarations of love for what she was learning, even her six-year-old silliness, opened a new door for him, a door to ready enjoyment and light-hearted humor.

SIDE NOTES

Hornbook

A hornbook is a wooden board upon which printed paper is mounted. It's called a hornbook because the paper is protected with a sheet of sheep's horn that has been boiled and scraped to make it pliable and transparent.

The Lord's Prayer on Anne's hornbook was taken from the Tyndale Bible, the first English translation. A later translation, the Geneva Bible, published in 1560 and dedicated to Queen Elizabeth I, was in Sir William's library but had not yet found its way to the making of a hornbook. It was a copy of the Geneva Bible that was presented to Oxford by his uncle, Arthur Golding, with instructions to mark passages in the book of Philippians—so that he could "begin to find true religion, true godliness, and true virtue."

The version of the Lord's Prayer most of us know today is from the King James Bible, which was published three-quarters of a century later.

Early Spelling

As the hornbook shows, spelling was not exactly like today's; there was no right and wrong—no dictionaries to consult. A word could be spelled more than one way even on the same page. Note the word *kyngdome* in line 3 and then in line 3-up with an extra *e* after the *g*. Note also the word *is* in line 5 spelled with a *y* and on line 3-up with an *i*.

Some of the irregularities in spelling came from changes in our alphabet. Back in Roman times, the letters J and U did not exist. The letter I served both as a vowel and as the consonant sound that the letter J now represents. The letter V also had two jobs—the one it still holds, as a consonant, as well as that of the letter U. The Romans spelled Julius Caesar's name like this: IVLIVS

Even in the 16th century the 26-letter alphabet was not firmly established. In the Tyndale Lord's Prayer, note the word *us*—with a *v* (lines 6, 7, 9, and 10).

Spelling was unstable. More than twenty different spellings are on record for Shakespeare.

Roman Arithmetic

Arabic numerals were new to England in Lord Burghley's day. He used Roman numerals. In Roman numerals, division is accomplished with repeated subtractions. Our own method of long division, which we learn in grade school, is just a formalized way of using repeated subtractions.   Repeated subtraction works well in Roman numerals, too.

Memory Tricks: How Small Anne Taught Herself Roman Numerals

        I = I, both are sticks
        II = 2 sticks
        III = 3 sticks
        V = the word five, with a big V
         IV = 1 less than V, that is, 4.
            On the Left
            a I = Less
         VI = 1 more than 5, that is, 6
            On the Right.
            a I = moRe
        VII = 5 plus 2, that is, 7
        VIII = 5 plus 3, that is, 8

X = 10, X TENd all fingers
IX = I less than 10, that is, 9
XI = I more than 10, that is, 11
XII = 12
XIII = 13
XIV = 14
XV = 15
XVI = 16
XVII = 17
XVIII = 18
XX = 20
IXX = 19
XXI = 21
XXX = 30
L = 50, haLf a hundred
XL = 40, X (10) less than L
LX = 60, X more than L
LXX = 70
LXXX = 80
C = 100, as in Centum
XC = 90
CX = 110
D = 500, a thousan-D
CD = 400, C less than D
M = 1000
over score = X 1000

CECIL AND MILDRED

Anne's mother's erect stance, red hair, and oval aristocratic face with high forehead, strong cheekbones, and shrewd, amber gaze intimidated most of the servants and tradesmen with whom she dealt. But her voice was musical, her smile was radiant, and her manifest devotion to her husband and daughter was fully returned by them. Nearly every evening when he returned from the Palace, Cecil went to her solar to discuss family and household matters.

On one occasion Lady Cecil spoke of his sons, her stepsons.

"Today William enjoyed his athletics— court tennis and curling," she said. "Robert did not enjoy studying Latin, but he is earnestly working at it, Oh, William, he is so like you, I do predict that someday he will be as valuable to the throne as you are."

Cecil described his morning with Anne and Oxford.

"Aye, William," Lady Cecil said, "After supper, Anne told me about her lessons. And then she astounded me by reading the evening lesson from the Book of Common Prayer. She knows how to read, William. I pray that she does not take up bookish, masculine ways. I am certainly pleased that you told her that His Lordship was jesting when he called her pretty."

"That was not the jest, my Mildred. The jest was that he said if she stayed so he would marry her."

"Now I am sore distressed. Anne must not think she is pretty. It is bad luck."

"But Mildred, she is an absolutely beautiful child."

"Aye, indeed, but never say so. It is a disability, even a curse. If she acts the proud, self-assured beauty, she will be feared by some who think beauty a gift of the devil. Others will see only vanity, and if she knows she is beautiful she cannot help but be vain. But if she thinks she is ill-favored, she will be humble and biddable."

"You want her neither bookish nor beautiful. I want her proud of her mind and aware of her beauty although modest about it. I am astonished that you should disagree with me on this. You are the model. You are comely and learned, and you have graced my life beyond measure. Without you, I could not hold my station with Her Majesty. You have been, you are, most valuable to me and our family.

"Surely, my Mildred, you would abhor being disgraced by a foolish, ignorant daughter. Surely you know there is nothing more irksome than a she-fool. Anne must stay true to herself and grow to be learned and sensible and lovely like her mother. The problem will be to marry her before . . . before she marries herself, for she has passion in her."

"Oh, William," she said, with tears in her voice, "I know I cannot think straight about that child. I want her to have a perfect life. She is beyond dear to me."

He put an arm around his wife's shoulders.

"As she is to me, and as you are to me. I remember, my Mildred, when we believed our marriage was solidly built on respect, but then we lost two children, and with the tragedy we discovered much more between us."

He took her hands in his and kissed the back of one after the other, slowly and thoughtfully.

"I believe we know something about passion, you and I," he said.

"Oh, William, indeed," she said. "And you have always had the skill to kindle the fire. You are skilled at many things—at everything you do. And you are right about Anne. You are always right. But I sometimes wish that once in a great while you would be wrong."

He turned her hands over and kissed each palm.

"I take it back; I like it that you are always right," she said.

1566: EMILY AND YOUNG VERE

Nurse Emily had begun her service in Cecil House at the age of eight as a scullery maid. When she was twelve, a young manservant taught her how to escape the eye of the housekeeper and earn a penny by hastily coupling with him in a closet or an unused bedroom. She soon learned how to please a man with less haste, soon expanded her clientele, and soon became pregnant.

She suffered a stillbirth the same week that Mildred, Lady Cecil, gave birth to Anne. The compassionate housekeeper called Lady Cecil's attention to Emily, and she became Anne's wet nurse.

Perhaps her mistress subconsciously recognized Emily as a less vivid version of herself with the same coloring and the same sharpness of face. In any event, Lady Cecil felt a connection, recognized that Emily showed great good nature and common sense, saw to it that she memorized the catechism, and saw further that she was promoted to full-time nurse after Anne was weaned, and to personal maid when Anne was thirteen.

And all the while Emily was covertly and cleverly expanding her carnal skills—and those of her clients, particularly those of the pubescent boys who lived at Cecil House as Sir William's wards, and most particularly young Vere. He had so charmed her (when he was but fifteen) that though he employed her services regularly she would accept no payment from him, neither money nor a gift of any kind.

When he was eighteen, however, she asked for a gift.

"That was a splendid romp, Emily," Vere had told her as he pulled up his nether stocks and his breeches. "I wish there was a way for me to express gratitude."

"There is a way. Would you—please—could you kiss me, my lord?" she whispered hesitantly. "Kiss me—give a kiss to me— like I am a lady."

"Nay, Emily, my Emmalina. 'Tis not fitting. 'Tis unseemly."

Oh Lud, he is a stuffed shirt, she thought. *I am daft over a boy stuffed with peacock feathers.*

"How so? I do not understand. You must make me understand. We have many happy romps. I know I am not a lady— the opposite—a drab, a harlot, bawd, whore—but not to you—not to you—from you no payment—I do not take payment from you. But—they say—all cats are black at night. When you bed me, how do I differ from a lady?"

"Emily," he said slowly, "I have never called you any of those names. I have greatly enjoyed your generosity, and I owe you much. "

She interrupted, "I think what you owe me is an explanation."

"Aye," he said. "Right, I will attempt it. Well then, here is my explanation, Emily. There are two kinds of lust. One, in holy matrimony, is for procreation. The other, for pleasure, is sinful. Clearly, I have inherited the proclivity toward sin. I do not often feel guilty, but sometimes I wish I were Catholic, so I could go to confession and be absolved."

Emily took his hands away from his eyes, pulled him down to the bed, and put her arms around him.

"Yes, now I understand—but My Lord—Surely, my lovely lord, procreation can be a pleasure.

"When you decide to marry, I will give you a wedding gift. You will teach your bride how to please *you*. I will show you how to please *her*. I will teach you rubbing and sidewise rocking and gyring and chair dancing and more. And you will kiss me in gratitude even if not on my lips."

"Can we begin now?" he asked.

Anne was a mature thirteen when the queen made her a lady-in-waiting. Her assignment was to taste the queen's morning and midday meals—some said to see that it was to Her Majesty's liking; others, to ensure that it was not poisoned. Anne knew that her father would not put her in danger, and performed the task happily.

The queen was easy to please. When Anne found fault with the food—perhaps because it was too salty or too dry or too ripe—the queen would say, "Let me try it," and usually then, "She's right, but I will eat it," or "I do not object. "Rarely, she would announce, "She's right. Send it back."

When the queen was away, her host would provide a food taster, and Anne would go home to spend time with her mother. That's where she was when the queen was spending the weekend in Devonshire to take part in match races with her favorite Irish horse, Midnight Rally.

Anne's father, having spent the weekend at the palace preparing a draft of Her Majesty's address to Parliament, sent Vere home to fetch fresh linen.

Vere went to Anne with the request. He was nineteen; his face still boyish despite a pencil-line of a mustache and a small goatee. His physique was strapping, his manner direct, and his presence commanding.

At court, Vere had seen how Anne's glowing look as a child was now even brighter, how her round face had changed to soft angular beauty, and how her body had developed womanly grace. When he saw her at home in her gown of deep blue velvet with triple-tiered emerald green damask sleeves, he was permanently besotted. He applauded, dropped to one knee, and sang to her, the chorus first:

> Greensleeves was all my joy,
> Greensleeves was my delight:
> Greensleeves was my heart of gold,
> And who but my Lady Greensleeves.
>
> Alas, my love, you do me wrong,
> To cast me off discourteously:
> And I have loved you so long
> Delighting in your company.

"Vere," said Anne, over her shoulder as she left to prepare the package for her father. "I know those words and I have danced to their music, but if you sing to me, you need new words because the old ones are nonsensical. I am sorely tempted to cast you off discourteously for I do dislike flirting!"

He was on his feet when Anne came back with the package and offered it to him, holding it in both hands,

He grasped both her hands, "I shall write new words," he said. "The song *Greensleeves* has particular meaning to me because my father wrote it."

"Don't bother with new words. I don't want to hear that sort of thing from you. Anyhow, I thought it was King Henry who wrote it," said Anne.

"I know many believe that, and indeed it was a favorite of his and he sang it and played it, but song-writing was not his talent. For example, he wrote a song with these unpoetic words:

Alas, what shall I do for love?
For love, alas, what shall I do?
Since now so kind
I do you find
To keep you me unto.
Alas!

"Not great poetry, is it? My father did better. He wrote *Greensleeves* when his first wife, Dorothy Neville, left him. He was a roué, my father, and she did not forgive him for that, but he loved her."

"I will write new words and sing them to you from my heart, my lady Greensleeves, and I hope you will like it."

He leaned across the package, pressed his lips against hers and quickly and lightly moved his tongue around the inside of her lips, laughed, took the package, and left her breathless and angry.

"You are hateful, my lord," she said, wiping her lips with the back of her hand.

"Ah, but you are lovable," he said as he left.

Lud, he has put me in a pother. Was it a joke? Do lovers act like that? she asked herself.

"Emily," Anne asked her maid, who had once been her nurse, "tell me about kissing. How do men kiss the women they love? Is it different from other kinds of kisses?"

"Now, now, child, you'll know soon enough—when you're older."

"Come now, the law says I've been old enough to marry for a year. You must tell me, does a man ever kiss a woman with his tongue?"

"Wherever have you heard of that filthy French custom? No English gentleman would do such a thing to a lady!"

She sought her mother.

"Madam," she asked, "tell me what lovers do in sexual congress. I know there is a physical union of male and female parts to make babies, but it is not the same as breeding animals because there is courtship. Tell me how kissing comes into it."

"Dear Anne, kissing does not come into it until you are in love and planning to be married, and then your husband-to-be teaches you everything you need to know about kissing, and finally, when you are married, about ... fondling and all the preliminaries to ... the union of parts. You will know all this soon enough—when you are married."

Fondling? Anne thought. *I have seen that with servants when they knew not I was watching. Well, if my mother is not going to explain kissing and those preliminaries, I will seek the information elsewhere; I shall look in the library. But I have worried my mother, so I must put her at ease.*

"How soon then, Madam, can I be married?" she said lightly.

Lady Cecil sighed in her relief at Anne's response.

"Whom did you have in mind?" she asked in jest.

"Well, not Lord Oxford, certainly," said Anne. "Not even when he is full grown and has more of a beard."

1570: GREENSLEEVES

It took two years for Vere to fulfill his promise to sing *Greensleeves* to Anne with new words. At Burghley's behest, he and his tutors had been sent away from Cecil House and the palace to his primary estate.

Then the queen granted Sir William the title of baron; he became Lord Burghley, and his wife became Lady Burghley. Anne, now a baron's daughter, was eligible to marry a nobleman.

And then Vere reached his majority. As was the custom for wards of the Crown, he sued for the return of his properties, which was promptly granted; whereupon, with his title, his estates, and his pride in his ancient heritage, he went to Burghley and offered for Anne.

"If she wants you, you have my full approval," said Burghley.

"I don't think she wants me. I want her," he said. "But she shows no sign of liking me except as a friend. She laughs at me when I give her compliments. She tells me to stop flirting."

Burghley took a deep breath. "My lord," he said, "A proper courtship is doing things together like taking tea and eating dinner and riding and dancing and going to the theater and taking Sunday walks on the green at Paddington. It is playing board games like draughts and card games like Triumph and talking just to get to know one another."

"We know one another. We have known each other for nearly ten years."

"Oh, this is an uncomfortable conversation. I am confounded; I don't know how to suggest that you pay court to my daughter."

"But you've courted a woman and won her."

"Aye, twice. But we are talking here about my own child, an innocent little girl. I cannot help you. It's too difficult. You might try talking to her mother."

Vere went to Lady Burghley and, after several minutes of small talk, he asked her outright, "My lady, I must come to the point. How can I win the reluctant Lady Anne?"

"Ah, so that is the point. Well, I could tell you, but I am uncertain that I should. I know you would listen because I would be entirely candid, and because what I say, coming from me, would be startling, even bold, and mayhap quite unladylike. I hesitate to do that."

"Please, my lady. I will be grateful. I will certainly think no less of you if you help me to my heart's great need. I do love your daughter. Please, my lady."

"My lady, you say. Well, I am a lady who wants a happy daughter. Very well. But you must not let anyone know that I have said these things."

"My word on it."

"Then here is my advice. Kiss her. Take your time. Kiss her sweetly and deliberately. First, kiss the back of her hands, one by one. Then, perhaps on another day, Turn her hands over and kiss her palms and then her wrists.

"Take her face in your hands and kiss her eyes, her temples, her cheeks, her nose, her chin, her ears, and at last, embrace her and kiss her lips. When you are sure she is willing, take her mouth."

"Pay no mind to the idea that a lady is too fragile, too refined for healthy lust. The idea is false. A husband and wife should know about passion. Your lady will prove as lusty as any gentleman if you are a gentle man and know what you are about. Wait for the wedding night, of course, for the final proof, and for discarding mistaken gentility, but before that time, make her eager.

"And close your mouth, my lord, I told you I would be frank."

"Thank you, madam, for your frankness. My mouth is closed," he said, and added in an aside, "Until I kiss Anne."

She responded angrily. "I heard that! You will not say such a bawdy thing in my presence ever again. I can easily end your chances with Anne, you know."

Your pardon, my lady." He spread his arms. "We have spoken of naught but the weather today. And in your presence from now on I will be the most gentle and genteel of gentlemen."

But her sense of mischief overcame her. "Until your wedding night," she said.

"I did not hear that," he said and bowed and left.

So Vere and Anne passed time alone together on occasions we would now call dates. She seemed to enjoy his company but pushes away his romantic overtures,

"I don't understand it," Burghley told his wife, "she treats him like a brother, not a suitor. At court, the girls and even older women react very differently. One young woman calls him her darling and says they belong together."

"He has good looks and great charm—natural charm that he hasn't yet learned to use, at least not with Anne," Lady Mildred replied "but maybe someone else will catch him before he does that."

Charm and sensitivity overcame the commonplace relationship, and Vere began to pay Anne muted compliments. "Good," or "Clever" or even "Wonderful" he would say when she told him what she had been writing or what she thought of something she was reading.

She started to listen to him seriously and to see his own ideas as bright and sensitive.

Then suddenly the wall fell, and she was so widely open to his courtship that he had difficulty following her mother's advice when she told him to "'take your time."

After a few days of romantic play, we come to an afternoon in which the smiling mother entered Anne's room carrying a box.

"Lord Oxford has asked me to bring you this," she said, "and to tell you to open it, put them on, and join him in the library."

The box was a yard long and a foot wide, its cloth of gold wrapping fastened by a pin enameled with the Oxford coat of arms.

"What on earth?" Anne asked.

She unpinned the wrapping, opened the box, and found a pair of sleeves made of pale green silk, heavily embroidered with deep green leaves and white flowers glowing with crystal dewdrops on golden branches.

"What an exceeding odd gift!" said Lady Burghley.

"Exceeding inventive!   He has called me Lady
Greensleeves, and has said his father wrote the song
Greensleeves," Anne said.

"The sleeves will look well on your new white gown. I
shall ring for Emily to help you dress," her mother said
"Take her to the library when you are ready."

Her mother, her father, her brother, and Vere's
uncle, Arthur Golding, were waiting with Vere when
Anne entered the library with Emily. Vere strode to her
and grasped her hands.

"New words," he said, and sang:

> Doubt thou the sun doth glow with fire,
> And doubt thy smile doth move me.
> Doubt thou the truth to be a liar
> But never doubt I love thee.
> Greensleeves is all my joy,
> Greensleeves is my delight:
> Greensleeves is my heart of gold,
> And who but my Lady Greensleeves.

He dropped to his knees.

"Dear Anne," he said, "I have been smitten by you
and lived with the wound for nearly ten years. Will you
mend my heart and marry me?"

Anne knelt by him

"It is my dearest wish," she said, "And will I then be
your countess?"

"Indeed," he said and took her in his arms, the two of
them knee to knee on the rushes covering the floor.

Burghley cleared his throat loudly.

"I know this is unsuitable for a suitor," said Vere,
"but I will have one kiss," and he took it gently and
sweetly before he helped Anne to her feet.

"Now I *have* to marry you," he said.

"Oh, good." she said.

Lady Burghley rolled up her eyes. Burghley exhaled a breath of relief. Arthur Golding, with his left arm around Vere and his right arm around Anne, said, "My blessings. May God be with you as the unseen friend and mutual lover, and may you forever remember that you first belong to Him."

"Amen," said Vere as he turned and held out his hand for his uncle to shake. To take Vere's hand Golding released Anne, and she stepped forward, stretched up onto her toes and kissed Vere's cheek.

"Now *I* have to marry *you*," she said.

"Oh, good," he laughed.

"Wicked child," said Lady Burghley.

"Behave yourself, Anne," said Burghley. "Remember who you are."

"Aye, Father, my Lord Burghley," she said, "I will behave perfectly from now on."

"Sorry to hear that," whispered Vere, "Because none of DeVere's holdings was ready for family living, Lord Burghley provided Anne with apartments in Cecil House—bed chamber, study, and sitting room.

It looked like a good marriage. Anne and Vere both, opinionated and loquacious. For a 15-year-old, she was well educated having been taught along with her brothers by an excellent tutor, and she was open to Vere's greater knowledge.

They were in love. They enjoyed being alone together, exchanging news, banter, ideas or warm silence. They both liked pudding and imported claret. They sang Lady Greensleeves together, blending her throaty contralto and his now and then out-of-tune rich tenor.

They enjoyed the same books and stories—especially Boccacio. They had certain ideas and values in common—such as their belief in courtesy and kindness to everyone, especially servants.

But they were very different in many ways.

Vere was a favorite dancing partner of the queen; Ann was privately scornful of dancing. He enjoyed the outdoors—riding, hunting, playing golf and lawn games (even the children's game of battledore and shuttlecock); she preferred the indoors and table games. He liked parties and the company of others; she liked being alone reading or working at her desk, and she quite disliked the role of hostess.

They argued often, quietly and stubbornly, and reconciled passionately.

For several months he came to her nearly every night, spending the days at Hampton Court Palace where he had his own room, ready to serve the queen, writing poetry, and attending to his remote properties by messenger, mail, and frequent visits from his hired managers.

Anne kept busy supervising her small staff, helping her mother prepare still-room medicines, cosmetics, jellies, wine, and beer. Best of all daytime activities (to her mind), were occasional dealings with her father, sometimes writing letters for him in her beautiful handwriting, sometimes translating his Roman-numeral accounts to the new-style Arabic numerals, proud that she knew both systems, and especially proud that she had done better than her brothers at the new arithmetic. And best of the best, whenever she saw him alone, hearing her father speak in confidence of the affairs of the queen and the court.

After the first few months, Vere found more and more reasons to take him from London or simply from Anne's apartments. He took workmen to make repairs at the Castle. He investigated ships in whose voyages he could invest. He published a book of his poetry. He attended court dances and country weekend parties.

She stayed home. She told herself she wanted to say home.

Then it became clear to her that, although he was discreet, faithfulness was not in his character; he was a libertine. She adapted; she quickly learned to play the role he seemed to want, that of innocently trusting wife.

The role did not suit her. Her disappointment, frustration, and general misery grew.

In their fourth year, after six weeks of his absence, she decided that her life would be improved by his permanent absence. She made her plans.

She asked her father to arrange a room for her near Vere's at the palace.

"Right, he said, "Good idea."

Once there, she arranged for her room to be directly across from his. That night she sat in her nightdress at her open door until he came.

When he saw her, he was thunderstruck.

"Anne. What ...?"

"Hush. Just follow me."

She led him to the bed, and welcomed him with full passion.

"Don't talk," she said, "Just show how you love me."

When they were sated, she remembered her plan and confronted him hotly.

"Why, why, Edward, is this not enough for you? Why must you stay away so long? Why must you stay away at all? Why must you have other women? Why am I not enough for you? Why, why?"

"Hush, Anne, my dearest," he said. "You are my wife. I love you deeply. Now I have something for you."

He got up, pulled on his breeches, left the room, and came back quickly with a string of pearls in her hand.

"I was going to bring these to you next month for your birthday," he said, "It's a gift worth a fortune, just as you are worth a fortune to me."

She looked scornfully at the pearls in her hand.

"If this really was intended for me," she said, "It's not anything I need."

"What then do you need?" he asked.

"I need a faithful husband who comes home to me nearly every night the way you used to. Can you give me that?"

"You don't understand. There's so much ... "

"Answer me. Can you give me what I say I need?"

"Well, not all of it. But let me explain."

"No lying explanations. I know the truth. I saw you with Emily. Why do you suppose she now works someplace else? Just the other day I was around a corner and overheard a woman I couldn't see advise someone else I couldn't see to get to know you because you are so good in bed. You are a reprobate, Vere, not a good husband. And you have stayed away and stayed away from your wife for days and weeks."

She drew a deep breath. "What do I need? I need you to go away and stay away now and forever," she stated firmly, "Just get out. Don't come back!"

She looked again at the necklace in her hand.

"I cannot believe you ever meant this for me," she said, and threw the pearls across the room.

He gasped in shock, shook his head in dismay, picked up the necklace, gathered his clothes, went to the door, turned and said, "As you wish. It's done," went out, and closed the door.

1576-1580: SEPARATION

She told herself she had no regrets. She was a mature nineteen years old, able to fill her life with worthy endeavors. She kept busy, shortening her previous routine and adding an entire afternoon of study, reading, and writing, content with being alone.

Evenings were particularly pleasant when her father had work for her—letters to write in her beautiful handwriting or accounts to convert from his Roman numerals to the Arabic arithmetic system in which she had done better than her brothers in school.

Then she found she would not be alone; she was with child. Joyfully she thought that bringing up a baby with no father would be the most worthy endeavor of all.

She wanted to read aloud to her unborn baby, but because her silent reading went too swiftly for that, she read aloud only slower documents—complex text, poetry, and her own writing.

Vere was miserable. He had been enchanted with Anne for more than a dozen years. She had discarded him, tossing aside a love gift worth a fortune. He went on a long, quiet binge.

After several months he heard of Anne's condition. "It certainly is not my child," he said. That night, at a dance at the palace, he embarrassed the queen by laughing too loudly, dancing wildly with several ladies, one of whom he applauded when she left him alone in the middle of the rows of dancers, and flirting openly with the giggling, young, unsophisticated wife of the Italian ambassador.

The next day Her Majesty strongly encouraged him to spend some time in Europe.

He was soon in Italy where he took a house and spent more than a year in wilder ways than any he had heard of in England.

1576: EMILY AND DICKEN

In July, Anne gave birth without incident to Elizabeth. Anne was entirely devoted; she nursed her baby and kept her clean and tended to her comfort, with her mother's loving help, for weeks. And then, inevitably, she saw that she wanted to go back to studying and writing part of the day. She needed a nursemaid, and she thought of Emily.

All through childhood and then through the early days of marriage, Anne had known Emily's exceptional care as nursemaid and personal maid. When she had silently seen Emily standing in a corner with Vere, reaching into his britches; she could not bear either to dismiss her outright or to accept her husband's libertine ways there in her own household. Her solution was simply to ignore the situation and find Emily another position in London. "Why are you sending me away, Mistress Anne?"

"Dear Emily. I think you know why."

"Oh—so you know—about me and His Lordship—Oh, I'm so sorry," she wept, "He's been special to me for a long time. It was wrong—I can't keep away from him. I can't help it, Mistress Anne—yet. But none the less, however, of course, you are still my dear—I can't help crying—My dear one, my dearest lady—You're right to send me away—I don't want to lose you—Oh, I know it has to be—I will never forget you—Aye. I have to leave— Oh. My Lady, I give you many, many thanks for your kindness about this, dear, dear Mistress Anne."

And that settled the matter. Then.

But later, after Vere's departure had removed the threat of his misconduct here, Anne offered Emily the position of nursemaid, with her sacred promise to keep strict social decorum. Emily happily came to work.

A problem soon became apparent. Dicken, Lord Burghley's chief footmen, who remembered their younger days of intimacy, would not let Emily alone.

Finally she asked the advice of her mistress.

"Tell His Lordship about this," Anne suggested, "but don't tell Dicken you've done that."

Emily told His Lordship.

"I'll take care of it," he said.

How he took care of it, saving a nursemaid's honor and keeping a good footman, shows why Her Majesty relied on him.

"Dicken," he said, "I have an added task to offer you. If you decide to do it, and do it well, I will consider a small raise in your pay.

"It involves Emily, the nursemaid who my daughter, Lady Oxford, has hired for my new grandchild. You may recall that she worked here for some time and was known by a few dishonorable staff members as—uh, an easy do. She has now promised to keep her— ah, integrity here .

"What I hope you will do is ensure that nobody takes advantage of her. I think you can do this from a distance, but if you must talk to her, always, always be sure that someone—ahem, someone impeccable is with you—to prevent rumor, of course. It's something I know I can trust you with. Will you take it on?"

Dicken was shaken with gratitude.

"Aye, Your Lordship," he said, "certainly, of course, truly, honestly, you can trust me, My Lord. I promise. Thank you, thank you."

1576-1600: VERE MAKES HIS WAY

Vere returned from Europe with an Italian choirboy, and set up housekeeping with him in Bradstreet.

Very soon, London associations, old and new, occupied Vere's talents and energies. He returned to more acceptable ways and sent Orazio back to Italy—to the relief of many friends and Lord Burghley. Now and for the rest of his life, he took an active part in the city's cultural life and entertainments.

He wrote and published poetry, and won an award. Here is an example of a colloquy between Vere and Philip Sydney (who was more foe than friend).

> Were I a king I might command content;
> Were I obscure unknown would be my cares,
> And were I dead no thoughts should me
> torment,
> Nor words, nor wrongs, nor love, nor hate, nor
> fears
> A doubtful choice of these things which to crave,
> A kingdom or a cottage or a grave.
> (signed)
> Vere

Sidney's Answer:

> Wert thou a King yet not command content,
> Since empire none thy mind could yet suffice,
> Wert thou obscure still cares would thee
> torment;
> But wert thou dead, all care and sorrow dies;
> An easy choice of these things which to crave,
> No kingdom nor a cottage but a grave.

He became a patron of many writers and writers and translators; thirty-three works were dedicated to him, including some on philosophy, medicine, music, religion, and literature—among which was Edmund Spenser's *Faerie Queen*. Several times he hired a writer to assist him in his affairs. He owned and helped manage several theater companies and acrobatic troupes. He wrote at least one play that was presented at court. He spent time at court, joining the Queen's and courtiers' games and amusements, often occupying his room at Hampton Court Palace. The Queen again made him a favorite dancing partner, and more—she invited him to be a companion on other court activities.

One day, after briefly embracing her as he lifted her from her carriage, he complimented her extravagantly, and asked if she would consider taking a lover.

"Oh, no!" she said, taking two steps away before turning back to explain.

"Edward, I choose virginity for life. I will never share my body with another. My body is private and pure, and therefore my mind is clearer, steadier, and broader than almost anyone else's. I am more than a woman; I am a Queen."

He bowed.

"Goodbye. Edward. I will see you tonight at the dance," she said.

And left his conscience released from the need to appear romantically faithful to Her Majesty. He could now respond to the overtures of several women at court, particularly to the avid invitations of Anne Vavasour, who had pursued him before his marriage.

Vere was not good at keeping his temper or saving money. A dozen or so bloody duels were fought by his men alone or with him. After one murderous affair, he had a permanent limp from a duel wound.

His investments often failed. Twice he lost great sums on ships that sank. He sold property after property to keep going. In later years, he was near bankruptcy, and in 1586 Queen Elizabeth granted him an annual stipend of one thousand pounds.

1576: BURGHLEY'S PLAN

"Tannakin," said Burghley, "Your daughter, my beloved grandchild, is a two-year-old female version of Edward De Vere, Lord Oxford. Her blonde hair arched on her forehead, her blue eyes with dark lashes, her chin, her smile—all reflect Vere.

"She should know her heritage. Once he sees her, cannot fail to recognize his paternity. What I plan to do is to take her to meet him."

"No, no," she said. "We do not need him. We are complete without him."

"You are mistaken, Tannakin. You are called a faithless wife by a few unkind people, and your child is known as illegitimate."

"Dear Lord," she wept. "I can't bear it. I had not thought of such dreadful things. Oh, I have been a fool, Father. Of course you must do as you plan. The sooner the better. For Elizabeth's sake."

"The sooner the better? Well, Tannakin, if you're certain, Vere is at his home in London today—as I am at home in Her Majesty's absence. I can take the child now."

Her eyes closed in resignation. "Take her, Father. Take her now. She's in the park with Clara. Clara takes her there every Tuesday afternoon."

"Clara, my first kitchen maid?"

"Oh yes. She's good with Elizabeth. They like each other. It gives Emily a short relief"

"Well, that solves a problem. It would not be wise to go to Vere with Emily."

"No, it wouldn't. Not that Vere would ... flirt, but Emily might. She's told me she can't help it: she finds him irresistible. 'Don't put us in the same room,' she once said.

"But I think you could take Emily to the park to find Clara and Elizabeth. She could take a basket with soap and water and a comb to clean up a little girl who has been playing in the park. And then Emily could walk back here while Clara goes with you."

He nodded. "Ring for her then."

In the carriage on the way to the park, Burghley explained to Emily his plan for young Elizabeth to meet Vere.

"If Lord Oxford admits his paternity, it may come to nothing in regard to your position with Lady Oxford," he said.

"But," he continued, "if there should be a change and a reunion—and I do have a small hope for that—I promise to find you a good position where you will be happy."

"My Lord, I thank you." she said, and then, speaking breathlessly, "But, well, I was going to tell Lady Oxford—but now—Oh, My Lord, I want to be married—I'm not too old to have children—Dicken has asked me—He doesn't talk to me much with other people being with us all the time, but he asked me—but I don't know how we can do it—because I want a house—because I could take care of young children there while their mothers work—in my house, that is—if Dicken and I had a house—if he could keep his job with you,—if he's not living here, that is—and Carol could take my job with Elizabeth—Carol is smarter than me—Carol can read and write—but I haven't figured out how we can do it—get married and live in a house, that is."

"Slow down, Emily. It's all right, Emily. I will speak to Dicken. We will work it all out."

He was laughing.

"Marry the man, Emily. Name your first son William, after me, and I'll see him through university.

"And hush," he responded to her effusive gratitude. "One thank you is enough. We have work ahead of us. And you must keep silent about this trip of mine to Vere with Elizabeth, and until I talk to Dicken, you must not talk about your own plans."

VERE'S PLAN

Waiting for Vere in his front hall, Burghley stepped aside to look at a painting by Breugel. When Vere entered he saw only Clara and a small girl child.

"What's this? Who's this?" he asked.

Elizabeth curtseyed and said, "I am Lydy Oxfud's bastid."

Burghley, overhearing, let out an agonized moan.

Clara hid her face in her hands and she cried out, "Oh, My Lord, My Lord, Jimmy in the park told her she should say that if anybody asked her who she was. I'm so sorry, so sorry."

Vere had caught sight of Burghley, and turned to him.

"This is Anne's child?"

"Yes, Vere. And yours, as you can see if you look at her, Just look at her. She's very like you."

Vere crouched in front of the little girl, removed her bonnet, and lifted her chin in his hand.

"She's certainly prettier than I ever was. Who is this wicked Jimmy?"" he said.

"Hello," said Elizabeth, smiling. "Did Jimmy do something wrong?"

He picked her up and sat her on a hall table

"I'll tell you in a minute," he said, and turned to Burghley.

"She's much too pretty to be called a bastard. I think I will accept her."

"Vere, she is yours."

"She can't be mine."

"When did you last—er, have relations with Anne?
"I know exactly, October second, 1574."
"Elizabeth was born on July second, 1575. —Count it. Exactly nine months."

Clara counted the months on her finger. "To the day!" she said.

Vere gulped and took a deep breath, stepped back and turned his head to wipe a few tears away with his handkerchief and came back to the child. He grasped one of Elizabeth's hands and told her, "Jimmy did wrong to say you are a bastid. The word is bastard, and a bastard is somebody without a papa."

"I don't know a papa. I have a grandpapa," she said

"What is your name?" he asked.

"Lizabet."

"Elizabeth, yes. That's your given name. What's your family name?"

She looked puzzled.

"Your surname, your last name."

"I don't know. Do I have more names?"

"Yes, you do. All right, you said you don't know a papa.

You do now, Elizabeth. I am your papa. You are my daughter, my own little girl, and you are Lady Elizabeth Devere."

Her eyes widened.

"I like that. You are my papa. I am Lady Lizabet DeVere. I want to hug you,"

She did that, and he hugged her back.

"I liked that too," she said.

"Lord help us. You are like your mother," he said, and picked her up and held her close.

"Vere," said Burghley, "Is there any chance of you and Anne coming together?"

"If there were, I would be there," Vere answered. "When we parted, she was as angry as anyone can become, and she infuriated me, but I miss her—deeply. I have loved her since the first day I met her. There has never been another woman so important to me and I long for her. If you think I have a chance ..."

"I'll look into it," sad Burghley. "I'll be in touch. Give me time."

"Time. I forgot that tonight I had so little. Burghley, I have an office back there full of waiting people. You have certainly accomplished your mission here with Elizabeth. I will formally acknowledge her as soon as possible."

"As for your mission with Anne, I hope for your success—my success also—as soon as possible. And now, blast it, I have to leave you for all those waiting people. When can I see my child again?"

"Clara takes her to the park every Tuesday afternoon."

"At two o'clock," said Clara.

"Next Tuesday then. I'll be there. Tell Anne, please, Burghley."

He kissed Elizabeth on both cheeks, said, "Goodbye Lady Elizabeth DeVere, Eliz, Liz, Lizabet, the dearest of the dear," and saw them out the door.

So began the tradition of Elizabeth Tuesdays, which he kept for the rest of his life, at first almost weekly and, in her adulthood, often monthly. Later children of his joined them or were given special times too, but, he said, "Elizabeth Tuesdays always shine."

Before he spoke to Anne about Vere, Burghley planned to wait for the passing of four Elizabeth Tuesdays. By then, he hoped that Elizabeth's enthusiasm about her days with her papa would warm her mama's heart.

Circumstance provided only three Tuesdays.

"Tannakin," he was obliged to tell her, "Her Majesty has sentenced your husband to a prison cell in the Tower."

"Tell me about it," said Anne.

She didn't ask, what's he done now? I'm pleased with her, he thought.

"Her Majesty is convinced that he fathered a child by one of her Ladies-of-the-Bedchamber."

"Anne Vavasour," said Anne.

"How in the world did you know that?"

"Easily. When I was there, half the ladies of the court pursued Vere, Father. And Anne was very persistent, shamelessly so. When she heard I was to marry him, she sobbed and sobbed. She said I was the most fortunate Anne in the world, the most honored woman of all time, and she was the most miserable because she so much wanted him, and she had tried so hard. She said she liked me too much to wish me dead, but she hoped something would happen to change things."

"Good Lord, Tannakin. I knew nothing of this.'

"She would not go to the wedding."

"Probably a good thing. She might have made a disturbance."

"Well, clearly, she waited till much later to do that. She finally caught him and managed to put him in prison."

"Tannakin! Your way of thinking shocks me."

I don't really mean it, she thought, *I liked her tremendously. She was a dear friend; I though of her as my other Anne. Some friends called us Anne C and Anne V. I still like her. But I have to talk this way because now she is an enemy.*

"I remember her wedding gift—a portrait of a woman, I suspect of herself so Vere would never forget her. It did look something like her, but it pictured a woman standing there in a white robe with her hands clasped, and I told him it was Saint Agnes, the Martyr. I never even let him know who gave it to us. It's in a storeroom. I should give it to the baby as a Baptismal gift. Or has Baptism already happened?"

"Oh yes. It has happened, Tannakin. That woman told Her Majesty she had to go to the country to care for her sick grandmother. That's where she bore the baby, and where she had him baptized Edward DeVere. Vere heard about it, left the court without permission, disappearing for a while, and when he was returned, tried to disclaim the child. Her Majesty sent for the Vavasour woman, questioned her and her friends, believed her story rather than Vere's, and put them both in cells in the Tower."

"She's with him in the Tower?"

"A long way from him. You know how big the place is."

"And where is the baby?"

"With the grandmother."

"Oh, Father, I hope Anne is well. I hope the baby boy is well cared for."

"Tannakin, please be angry, not kindly and caring. You should be concerned that the new baby's name spoils any chance of a son of your own—should you reestablish yourself with Vere—any chance of your son being the heir."

"You could mend that, Father."

Aye, I could, he thought.

"What I am concerned about now, father, is what to do today, right at this time."

She hid her face in an agony of emotion.

"I've made such a mess of it for Vere—putting him in that other Anne's path. What can I do? What should I do? "she sobbed. "Elizabeth told me Vere said mamas and papas belong together. But there are too many mamas for this papa."

And the new baby will have a good mama, she thought. *If only Vere could be persuaded to be a good papa to both children while he belongs only to one of the mothers—me. For that's what my heart says should be.*

Burghley picked her up in his arms, saying. "'My Tannakin, we'll go to your mother, and together we'll figure out what to do."

He carried her down the hall to Lady Mildred's workroom, where he knew she would be embroidering a pillow for a wedding gift (in addition to money) for Emily and Dicken). There he sat Anne in a chair, and told his wife why they had come.

"Dearest William," she said, "You are a wonderful father, and a very good man, but this is woman's business. So, please, my dear, leave us alone now."

She beckoned him to her, kissed him, told him she would keep him informed, and waved from the room.

Later, this is what she reported to him:

"Anne is distressed, of course, that Vere is incarcerated, although she knows it will not be for long. Before we talked, she did not know what to do when he is released. She thought the reasons she sent him away were still valid—his long absences and his unfaithfulness—but she longs for him—both for herself and for Elizabeth.

"I told her some things she had not realized. First of all, she had lived *here*, in the home of her father, the queen's councilor. It was her own apartment, indeed, but it was not Vere's home. And she had seen none of his properties and had performed no wifely duties with any of them. She had kept her own life, reading, writing, writing, writing, and had done little to enter his. She had not behaved as the Countess of Oxford.

"Next, I told her that she had grown up with you as a model of what a husband is, and she had seen nothing of other husbands. Vere's model, however, was his father, as renegade a husband as ever was.

"Then I reminded her that women do pursue Vere, and sometimes may catch him, but I pointed out that that had never meant she was not his only true love— which is what she is.

"I knew it when Elizabeth sang *Greensleeves* to me with his loving words: He told her not to sing the song to her mama until he was there with them. So she sang it to me, her grandmamma."

Lady Mildred sang the words:

Greensleeves is all my joy,
Greensleeves is my delight:
Greensleeves is my heart of gold
And who but my Lizabet's mama.

At his look, she said, "No. William, I did not sing it to Anne. I kept Vere's condition. I sang it now to show you how I know Vere's feelings.

"And Anne and I made a four-point plan," she continued, "First, She will send food to him every day. "

"Good!" he interrupted. "The cook does not provide prisoners with the most savory of meals."

"I've heard that. So every day Anne will send good food to his cell. Today a note will go with it informing him about Elizabeth—that she has been told he is sick in a hospital where the care is good but the food is inadequate, and that she sends best wishes for his happy tummy.

"Second, when he is released, Anne will ask to share an Elizabeth Tuesday with him. Third, she wants you and me to invite him to dinner with her and Elizabeth, and of course we'll do that. Fourth, she will request his help with a piece she is writing, a drama with a ghost, she said, which would put them together several times— enough, she hopes, to unite them husband's side."

1576: HEARTS RIGHTSIDE UP

On a Friday that happened to be the one before Vere was released, Emily Flinders became Mrs. Archibald Bartholomew Cornelius Dicken in a small ceremony in the Cecil House chapel. Emily's attendant was her sister, Belle, whom she had not seen for years and did not know had become a streetwalker. (She never did discover that.)

As soon as Belle entered Cecil House, the butler took her to a side parlor, called Lady Mildred, and warned her she had a problem in that room. Mildred took the problem's hand, asked her to come along, showed her to one of her own rooms, fitted a bonnet over the dyed hair, removed the heavy makeup and large ear dangles, dressed her in dark conservative clothes, put a string of black-painted beads around her neck, and had her look in a full length mirror. Nell saw an elegantly pretty woman.

"Lud, if I look like this I can catch a banker," she said.

"Well, if you're looking for a husband, six unmarried footmen are coming to the wedding. But remember, if you want to catch a husband, you must let the man make all the physical advances."

"Nay, really? Nay!"

"Aye, believe me! And you should also know that the best place to find a husband is in church, an unmarried singer in a chorus, maybe."

No footman was taken with Emily's respectable-looking sister. Some months later, however, she did catch a widowed church singer, a bass, who made a fair living at a local bank as a guard.

Dicken's best man was his father, who distinguished himself by offering a tipsy toast.

Burghley introduced him, "May I present the groom's father, who gave me his card to read to you: Samuel, Dicken Tailor and Clothier of Fine Gentlemen. Deign, Production, Renewal, Repair. If you want his address, I'll be glad to provide it privately. Mr. Dicken?"

After too much unaccustomed champagne, he rose shakily to his feet, opened a paper, held it in one hand, raised his glass in the other, and read, looking up for parenthetical remarks.

"A Taste from a Toler. (Toast from a Tailor, that is.) May joy spread through whatever you do. (ah, that's wrong. may joy THREAD through whatever you do), and   may love's rich invisibubble, invisibibble, invincible (that's a good one) may   love's rich INVISIBLE stitches, (and that's the kind I stitch, invisible, with a needle so fast it's nearly invisible too. ha ha.). Well, may love's (ho! I just thought: of a play on words—not in-vis-i-ble, but   inDIVisible) stitches repair life's wear and tear.

"My wife wrote that poem, but I want to add this: To Archie and Evelyn, what is it, Sugarheart? Oh, sorry, it's EMILY! To Emily but especially to Archibald, May your marriage be as happy as your mother's ... and mine, of course ... as happy as MINE and your mother's was ... IS! Lord help me, Sugarheart, I can't get it right but you know very well that I love you."

And you know I love you, Sam," said Sugarheart, "Now sit down, my dear."

Sam sat down, bent his head, and fell asleep.

The company silently watched Sugarheart rise and make her swift way to her husband's side.

She spoke with great clarity.

"Sam said, 'You know I love you.' and I could easily have answered with just 'Aye, I know.' But I said the same back to him because our forty years together has indeed been very good, wear and tear included. And here, at this wonderful wedding, we wish you, Archy and Emily, as good a marriage as ours is. Now here is my poem—A Toast from a Tailor:

> May joy thread through
> all that you do,
> and may love's rich
> invisible stitches
> neatly repair
> life's wear and tear.".

She nodded and went back to her place at the table
The applause was wildly enthusiastic.

1581-1587: REUNION

Vere was released on a Saturday (a week before Anne Vavasour was released to receive official notice that she was also released from her position at court).

Upon Vere's release, Anne's second and third plans were immediately overthrown. The fourth came later. Vere invited his estranged wife, his daughter, his in-laws, and his half-uncle Arthur Golding to his house in London for "an entertainment" on the coming Tuesday afternoon, an Elizabeth Tuesday.

As the entertainment, he had Elizabeth sing this:

> Greensleeves is all my joy,
> Greensleeves is my delight:
> Greensleeves is my heart of gold
> And who but my Lizabet's mama.

Then he sang this:

> Greensleeves or red or blue
> her sleeves can be of any hue,
> Her self entire is my heart of gold
> and who but yourself,
> dearest Anne.

After he sang, he dropped to his knees.

"Dear, dearest Anne," he said, "I have been smitten by you and lived with the wound for nearly twenty years. Will you mend my heart and stay here and live with me?"

Anne knelt by him

"It is my dearest wish," she said, "And I will then be your countess indeed."

"Indeed?" He said, "Indeed!" and, holding her in his arms kissed her deeply, the two of them knee to knee on the rushes covering the floor.

Burghley exhaled a breath of relief.

Arthur Golding raised his arms, put one around Vere and the other around Anne, and said, "I understand now why I am heed, to give you my blessings as I gave them to you before, and now they are even stronger. May God always be with you; may you never forget that you first belong to Him; and may your years with Him and each other and your children be long and happy."

Four voices spoke resounding amens.

"Me too," said Elizabeth, "amen, amen."

PROMISES

After a few weeks of settling into Vere's home, Anne adapted to her role as Countess gracefully, and happily.

What made the renewal of her marriage most meaningful to her, however, was what Vere had told her on the first night she spent in his—now also her—home.

"Anne. let me tell you how you have changed my life," he began.

"It starts as a sorry tale, and painful.

"When I was a child, I think about seven years old, I overheard my mother talking to my father.

"She was weeping. She thanked him for asking, but she could not welcome him to her bed that night. She said that God required a wife to submit to her husband for procreation, not for pleasure, and that she had done her duty years ago.

"She said, and I think I remember the very words. 'My Lord, you have your heir. Forty-eight hours I labored to give you Edward. He made me scream with the agony of birth—and screaming is a thing no lady should ever have to do. It happened also with the birth of Mary. I cannot abide the thought of birthing another child. Mothering is hard enough, I endure Mary because she is a girl, but I cannot care for Edward, who challenges me and argues about politics and religion and other things no child should be concerned with.'

"My father spoke quietly and said something like this: 'God's wounds, Madam, you do not see that the boy is remarkable. He inspires devotion in all who serve him.

I am marvelous proud of him. But you, madam, I have nary a whit of admiration for such a mother or of enthusiasm for such a wife. Never again shall I trouble you,' he said.

"I never again gave my mother more than short simple politeness.

"So that is why she was not overborne with grief when my father died and I was taken away as Sir William's ward. I have not seen her since my father's funeral. She has never sought me. Mary I have seen now and then, but she is a shrew and I avoid her. The other member of the family, Arthur Golding, my mother's brother, has always been close. I'm fortunate to have Uncle Arthur in my life.

"I have heard that my father was wickedly profligate. He treated my mother with cold courtesy, but he was ever solicitous of me.

"The point is this: I thought lying with a woman was a sin. I have a proclivity for the pleasures of that sin, I admit, but when I married you I learned that the act—with you—is not sin but love-making—making our love real, a practical reality, a means to fulfill us beyond the idea or ideal of love. That's what you have done to me."

"Vere. Vere, my dear dear Vere," Anne said. "I am happy and grateful to hear what you say. But—and it's a large *but*—I suspect that our sinless love-making lessened the sin with other women. You have been immoral, Vere: In spite of that, I do love you with all my heart, and now that we are together, I will forget the past. But—again a *but*—what will our future be?

She has no idea of the extent of my immoral past, thank God. And may God forgive me for thanking Him, as well as for my immoral past, he thought.

"Although the temptations are often very great, my Anne," he answered, "Uncle Arthur's teachings about sin have come home, and I promise to try mightily to be faithful. If a lady at court sidles up and collides against me with her hip, I'll shout, 'Ouch! Look out!' and if one rubs my arm or my cheek, I'll make a face as if she stank and say, 'Please do not touch me!' And I promise firmly never again to be tempted by Emily or Anne V."

"Well then," she responded, "I promise to try mightily not to be tempted by any of the foreign dignitaries or members of Parliament to whom papa introduces me, or to be tempted by a good-looking actor n one of your theaters."

"Agreed," he laughed, "Let's shake hands on it."

"Oh, I think we might go a little further than a handshake," she said.

INSURANCE

Anne persuaded Burghley to turn over several rooms of the apartment she would be leaving to Emily and Dicken. They then would be near enough for Dicken to perform his usual duties easily, and far enough away to give Burghley privacy and to keep Emily's venture into childcare out of his purview.

"But," Anne told Emily, "you will lose your home if you ever again misbehave with Lord Oxford."

"Oh my lady, no fear, "Emily responded. "No fear at all my lady, no fear whatever... I am a wife...with a husband...a good husband...a very very good husband."

Anne could not resist repeating this conversation to Vere.

"So, Vere dear," she asked, "what threat can I make to be sure Anne V never again pursues you?"

"No need, Anne, love, no need at all, no need whatever. Anne V is in hot pursuit of another lord— and I once felt that heat. But it will never again burn me. And were that to change, I would spurn her. The idea turns my stomach. I tell you, I was highly relieved to be free of her clinging ways, her pats and rubbings and touchings."

Anne took her hand from his arm. He grasped it, kissed it, and gently put it back on his arm.

"Anne C, Lady Anne, Lady Oxford, my beloved," he said, "*your* touch is always welcome."

MUTUAL APPROBATION

Anne and Vere had shared much of their lives and learning with each other, and their writing styles were very similar—vocabulary, conciseness, and emotion ready for the rhythm and color of speech. They did not, however, recognize this similarity.

They never wondered why their regular "Tuesday Two-Way Reviews" were full of applause for each other's work. Once in a while one or the other would confidently suggest a small change, and the change would be accepted immediately—with thanks, never with an argument. Here are examples:

One of the changes to Vere's work is on record. Vere had ended a verse of a poem with this couplet:

> And he that beats the bush
> the wished bird not gets
> But such, I see, as sitteth still
> and holds the fowling nets.

Vere improved it by shortening the lines—as Anne had suggested.

> And he that beats the bush
> the bird not gets,
> but who sits still
> and holdeth fast the nets.

One of Vere's changes to Anne's work is now a famous quotation:

> The quality of mercy is not strained
> It droppeth as the gentle rain from heaven.

Anne had written, "The quality of mercy. . . falleth as the gentle rain...." She quickly agreed when Vere

commented that falling mercy might be somewhat
unmerciful.

1587: PUSSY CAT, PUSSY CAT

One day, Vere arranged for Anne and 3-1/2-year-old Bridget to join him and 12-year-old Lizabet for a Lizabet Tuesday morning. In the children's playroom he turned to Lizabet (now twelve years old) and asked, "Pussy Cat, Pussy Cat, Where have you been?"

Lizabet instantly understood and answered, "Meow! I've been to London to visit the Queen."

Vere turned to Bridget. "Pussy Cat, Pussy Cat, what did you there?" he asked.

She followed her sister's example, answering,

"Meow! I fwightened a little mouse under her chair."

"Excellent!" he said. "That rhyme tells a little story about a cat and a mouse. And there's a bigger story behind the little one. Your mother will tell it to you."

Anne nodded and smiled. "It's a good story," she said. "It goes back to when I was a little older than Lizabet, serving as a lady-in-waiting to Her Royal Majesty."

"Will I ever get to be one of those?" interrupted Lizabet.

"I've been thinking about it," answered her mother.

"If you wish it," said Vere, "Your grandfather can assure it."

"II think I wish it," said Lizabet. "I wish to be a lady-in-waiting to the queen."

"Me too," said Bridget.

"I hear you," said Vere, "I will take care of it.

And now back to the pussy cat."

Anne took over. "I saw him first, matted and scrawny, in the corridor with a footman yielding a broom, to sweep him out the door.

"I rescued him, took him to my room, brushed him, cleaned him, fed him, saw what a pretty, fluffy gray puss he was, and named him Tommy.

"We set up a routine. Every morning, I would let Tommy out the door to the gardens. After the noon meal, he would be waiting on the foot of my bed; he would eat the food I brought, we would take a nap, and I would let him outside again. At bedtime he would be there; I would groom him, and we would spend the night together.

"In between times, once in a while I would see him in a garden or a hallway or a room, but he was generally unfriendly, even to me, and generally inconspicuous.

"The great event happened in one of the palace's living rooms. Picture the room as if you were there as I was.

"I was there because cakes and ale were to be served, and I was Her Majesty's food taster."

Vere told them, "I was there with my sister, your Aunt Mary, because that's how I could meet her demand to meet the queen."

Anne continued, gesturing as she spoke. "It's a living room that Her Majesty uses for small social events. Around the room are two sofas and four pairs of chairs with little tables between them, and in the middle is an elegant chair with a high ornate back—the queen's chair, known as "The Chair." Across the room from The Chair is the door to the room. On this day the guest chairs were filled. I was standing in a corner behind the guests." "Mary and I were on a sofa," said Vere.

"Her Majesty entered, walking with a cane. The guests stood up. Standing beside her chair, she motioned them down, smiling, ready to say words of welcome when from the   door—horror of horrors— Tommy hurtled, chasing a mouse that squealed in fear all the way across to the royal chair. Under The Chair, Tommy caught the mouse in his mouth, let it go briefly, caught it again, this time in his paws, and began to play with it. He pawed it, sniffed it, and let it go. The mouse stopped squealing and ran away. Tommy stretches a long front leg and caught it. The mouse squealed as he pawed and sniffed it. He let it go, and the mouse quieted and ran, Tommy caught it, and the whole sequence began again. The onlookers were horrified. A few seemed paralyzed, but most stood up to watch. A man's shouted, 'Catch the cat. Destroy the cat.' Voices took up a chant 'Drown the cat, Drown the cat.' A woman screamed, 'He's under Her Majesty's chair. It's treason. Execute him!'"

"That was my sister," said Vere.

Anne went on. "I ran through the hubbub, knelt by The Chair, reached down, and picked up Tommy as the cat was holding the mouse in his paws. A footman— with some difficulty—got the mouse away from Tommy and hurried out the   door with it. The queen waved goodbye to the mouse, bent down and, with her cane, made sure the floor under her chair was clear. Then she sat down, and spoke.

'I was about to make a small speech of warm welcome to each of you, one by one, when   this unscheduled, unwelcome, unseemly event occurred. I apologize deeply for the intrusion. Now, does anyone know anything about this cat?'

"I was sitting on the floor by the chair with Tommy on my lap.

I answered, "Oh yes, Your Majesty. He's my cat. He's a good cat. His name is Tommy. Please let me keep him."

"Our Gracious Queen put her hand on Tommy's head and spoke to the assembly:"

'This is Tommy. He belongs to lady Ann Cecil, a Lady-in-Waiting. She says he is a good cat. It doesn't matter that he's good. He's a cat. He is unable to distinguish between treason and disrespect; he doesn't know what either means. He's a cat. He knows nothing of royalty, and he never will. Much of his behavior comes from instinct. His instinct tells him to chase mice. In fact, I shall make it his duty.

'Tommy, I now pronounce your sentence. As long as you chase mice, you have my authorization to run free. Now, Anne, take him away.'

"I put him out the door, and he ran free as if to chase mice.

"Now this is the whole rhyme:

> "Pussy Cat, Pussy Cat,
> Where have you been?"
> "I've been to London
> to visit the queen."
> "Pussy Cat, Pussy Cat,
> What did you there?"
> "I frightened a little mouse
> under the chair—
> 'Drown the cat! Drown the cat!'
> everyone cried,
> 'His crime deserves that.'

But the queen took my side.
'Pussy Cat, Pussy Cat,'
was her decree.
'You keep chasing mice, and
you keep running free.'

"The end," Anne said, and bowed deeply.

Vere and Lizabet applauded.

Bridget said, "Thank you, Mama. What happened to Tommy?"

"Well," Anne answered, "For quite a while, we went on as before, spending time together every day and night. And then one afternoon he didn't come. I looked all around; I asked anyone I saw.

"I didn't give up the search for days, but he just disappeared. I like to think he joined a herd of cats and is playing games and chasing small creatures in the forest."

"What happen to the mouse?" asked Bridget.   *Oh dear. I'm sure the footman drowned him,*   thought Anne. But she answered, "I would   imagine the footman kept him in a cage as a pet."

"Can we have a mouse?" Bridget asked.

"No!" stated Vere. "No mice allowed here."

"Can we have a cat as a pet?" asked Lizabet. "I think I would like to have a cat."

"A cat! Me too" proclaimed Bridget.

"I'll look into it," Vere responded.

PLANS FOR A CELEBRATION

Lizabet took the opportunity on a Tuesday with her father to suggest that they begin to plan for her mother's thirty-second birthday celebration.

She sat with the family's new black kitten on her lap, and told him that she thought they should have an afternoon party rather than a dinner because it would be a good time of day for Bridget and eight–month-old Susan.

She said that an entire family gathering should include her grandparents, uncles, aunts, and cousins, and certainly the portraits of her baby brother who had died in infancy four years ago, and baby Frances, who had died in September.

Vere struck this notion down when she had barely begun to express it.

"No, Lizabet, No! No, Lizabet, No! Your grandfather and grandmother, certainly;   Bridget and Susan, indeed. Nobody else. Your mother dislikes large parties. "

"Not even Uncle Arthur?"

"All right, Uncle Arthur, and that's it. As for the babies in heaven, do not even mention the names, Lord Bullabecke and Lady Frances!"

"Why, why? She loved them. She treasures their memory."

"That may be. But I think you never heard her mention one of their names after they died. Now hear," he said, and went to his desk, "I'll read you something she wrote about the boy's death."

He unlocked a desk drawer, took out a paper and
read this:

> Oh Destiny,
> you might rather have taken,
> my twenty years:
> than the two days of my dear son.
> And what then shall I hope,
> because I know,
> the world, in his respect,
> yields naught but moss:
> Or what should I consume
> but more in woe,
> when Destiny, and Gods,
> and all my worlds,
> are joined here in my loss.

With tears in her eyes Lizabet gulped and said,
"Destiny and God and all her worlds. I see. Oh, yes, I do
see. A reminder of sad memories would be wrong and
out of place. The party is a celebration. We must keep it
fun."

"And keep it small, "I'll do the invitations," said Vere.
"I'll do the program," said Lizabet..

THE PARTY

Lizabet adapted two songs and enlisted her father, grandparents, and Uncle Arthur to perform the accompanying actions, imitating her as she conducted.

At the party when food and drink were finished, this is how the program went:

Bridget sang in her sweet soprano as the group silently moved to the beat, imitating the actions of Lizabet.

<u>Alphabet Song</u>
Bridget: A B C D E F G
Group: (nods up down, up down, up down, up)
Bridget: H I J K L M N O P
Group: (turn heads left, right, L R, L R, L)
Bridget: Q R S and T U V
Group: (shrugs up down, up down, up, down, up)
Bridget: double you X Y and zed
Group; (hands cover eyes, uncover, cover)
Bridget: Now I've said my ABCs
Group: (claps hands silently 4 times)
Bridget: I ask that you reward me, please
Group: (throws kisses left, right, left, right)

Anne and baby Susan (with her mother's help) threw kisses back.

This time Bridget's grandmother, Lady Mildred, put Bridget in a chair, stood behind *her, and sang the* words as the child just hummed. And this time the group of three men, imitating Lizabet, held exaggerated facial contortions for a full line of the song.

<u>NUMBER SONG</u> (same tune as Alphabet Song)
Singers: 1 2 3 4 5 6 sev'n   :
Group: (left side of faces screwed)

Singers: 8 9 10 and then elev'n
Group: (right sides screwed)
Singers: 12 13 14 15
Group: (both cheeks puffed)
Singers: 16 17 18 19
Group: (faces contorted as for very bad smell)
Singers: 20 21 23 and 4
Group: (sad weepy faces)
Singers: and many many numbers more
Group: (huge open mouth grins)

Anne laughed and laughed and cried and applauded and applauded. The household onlookers applauded too. Except baby Susan, who yawned and squirmed.

For the crowning act, produced by Vere, Lady Burghley played the spinet, and Lizabet and Bridget, held by her grandfather, joined the performers.

BIRTHDAY SONG (to the tune of Green sleeves)
Vere: Today's a very special date
          For all of us to celebrate
          Together here we congratulate
          Ladies Green sleeves, Oxford,
              and Anne.
ALL: A happy birthday to you to you,
          happy happy birthday to you to you.
          A happy birthday to you to you.
Three girls: Happy birthday to you,
          my dear Mother.
Parents: Happy birthday to you, my dear
              daughter
Vere: Happy birthday to you" my dear wife.
All: Happy days for the whole of your life.

Anne got up, hugged each performer, and asked them, "Now everybody sit down and be the audience while I make a speech."

"Any one of you," she said, "is as great an actor as any Vere has hired, and I thank you deeply for displaying such extraordinary talent for me. But today it is not my birthday I celebrate. Today and every day I celebrate my glorious connection with you—with you, my marvelous family."

"Now imitate me," she said, waving goodbye as she walked to the door of the room. Her audience waved back while she sang impromptu words to an impromptu melody,

<u>GOOD NIGHT SONG</u>
Anne: Good night, good night, good night.
Parting is such sweet sorrow,
but I must leave you now and say
goodbye until tomorrow."

Lizabet leapt up, faced the others, sang "Goodbye until tomorrow," and, like a conductor, motioned to the group to do the same.

As Anne left the room, she was followed by a ragged chorus singing "Goodbye until tomorrow."

Anne came home early from shopping because she was tired of swollen ankles, tired of feeling ill all day, tired of worrying that this baby would be another girl instead of heir to the title, tired of being tired.

The laughter in the small parlor lured her. She opened the door quietly and saw Lyly, Marlowe, Kyd, Raleigh, and her husband sitting in a half circle of chairs, watching and listening to a young man who was declaiming:

> Give few thy voice but every man thy ear,
> Take each man's judgment,
> but reserve thy own.
> As costly make thy habit as thy purse can buy,
> But rich, not gaudy; nothing fanciful,
> For his apparel oft proclaims the man.
> Neither a borrower nor a lender be;
> For loans oft lose friends and themselves,
> And borrowing begets improvidence.

As he spoke, he nodded; he gestured with his left hand; he waited just a shade too long between thoughts. He smiled and blinked when the words were particularly apt. He took a step sideways and then a step back.

His mannerisms were all too familiar. It was an unmistakable parody of Lord Burghley. The actor continued:

> This above all: to thine own self be true,
> And it must follow, as the night the day .

"Stop!" she cried. Vere and his friends turned, saw her, and stood up and bowed, as gentlemen do in the presence of a lady.

"Who in the name of all that is holy are you?" she asked the actor.

He shrugged and looked questioningly at Vere.

"Tell her, Will," said Vere.

"I am Polonius, my lady," he said.

"You should be ashamed, Polonius, mimicking Lord Burghley, the Lord Treasurer so offensively. Please, Vere, I would speak to you in private," she said, beckoning.

"Excuse me, gentlemen," he said, and went out with her to the hall.

"How could you? How could you permit someone so to mock my father? And all of you laughing! As if it were ridiculous. As if he were ridiculous."

"You wrote it, Anne. You wrote the words."

"Not as a parody, not as a joke, but as sensible advice from a wise old man. And the words— not all are mine. I wrote, 'Rich, not garish,' and *garish* became *gaudy*. I wrote, "not whimsical." It became 'not fanciful.' I wrote, 'Borrow not from nor lend to anyone.' You changed it too."

"I did, aye, for the better, I thought, and I hope you will forgive me. But Anne, it is your father to the life. You have written a close portrayal. I'm sorry you saw it. You were not meant to," he said, "But 'tis a fine performance Will gives. And the speech—it is indeed ridiculous—ridiculous and wise at once. As for the advice, it is the same your father gave to you and your brothers. I remember his saying that courtesy towards one's equals makes one known as well-bred, I remember when he advised Thomas not to borrow money."

"I am not offended by your changes. As always, they are improvements. But I am offended that you arranged a reading without asking me. I am even more offended that the young actor was mocking the Queen's Lord Treasurer. He should be in the Tower. Send him away. Send them all away at once."

"They are my friends."

"Not mine. I want them out of my house."

"It is *my* house, Anne."

"Indeed. And do you wish me to stay in it?"

"Of course. So go up and wait for me. Sleep. Bathe. Drink a soothing posset. Write me an angry letter. Do what is needful to calm yourself or the babe will suffer."

He came to her after an hour.

"Are they gone?" she asked from the bed.

"Aye."

"Have you told them they can never come here again?"

"Nay."

"Will you do that?"

"Nay."

"Vere, you are a monster, a cruel, spiteful monster. I'm full of anger. I will not have my father made into a jest."

"I love you, Anne," he said, taking her hands, "And you love me."

He kissed the back of each hand.

"Vere, I don't wish to love you; you build a barrier between us when you make sport of my work. You never did that before. You approved of it. But now you have constructed a barrier."

"Oh nay," ha said, "Let me not to the marriage of true minds admit impediments."

His words captured her. "That sounds like the beginning of a poem," she said.

He took a deep breath "It is. The words begin a sonnet, one of several in manuscript that I have only polished and corrected. The original was written by the young actor you met, Will Shakespeare, who called himself Polonius. Let me not to the marriage of true minds admit impediments. Love is not love which alters when it alteration finds, Love alters not..."

He kissed the palm of her left hand.

"Enough," she said. "Love alters not. I know what those words mean."

"Oh God, I do too. We both know about alteration," he said, and kissed the palm of her right hand.

"And still we love," he said, and drew her, now willing, to him.

MEANING

Anne miscarried. When she had recovered her physical health, she also seemed to have recovered her usual cheerfulness. But she began sleepwalking.

After Vere had found her several times at odd corners of the house in the middle of the night, he hung a bell on her bedroom door to alert him when she wandered.

One night he carried her back to bed, woke her, and asked. "Anne, love, you have been sleepwalking. What are you searching for?"

"I didn't know I did that. Maybe I'm searching for what I always search for—words, good words to put on paper.

"Vere, dear Vere, I had sent you away, and you didn't know that when I gave birth to Lizabet I had an astounding revelation. I knew this was what I was meant for I knew the very meaning of my being was to produce a child and to nurture it.

"Then, after we came together again, I lost two babies, a darling boy who would have been your heir and a sweet girl, and this year I lost a seedling that never came to fruition.

"Certainly, of course, unquestionably, I deeply love our three wonderful daughters, but I quite lost my meaning. Until lately.

"Lately I have found a broader meaning. I can tell you about it now that I am sure of it All my life I have been writing to fill my spirit. Now, with your aid and that of actors like Will Shakespeare, I see that I have been writing for performance. My meaning is in my pen."

He nodded. "Bravo," he said, "and your meaning to me is in my heart."

The following night he heard the warning bell. In his haste to help the sleepwalker, he fell out of bed and sprained his ankle. Limping out his door, he saw Anne on the top step of the great stairway, grasping the banister as if about to descend.

"Anne, take care," he called, She turned, took a step, and fell out of sight.

He stumbled forward from the closed hallway to the open area overlooking the front entry room. Grasping the railing atop the fence posts that continued down the staircase, he looked below. There she was, lying on the floor at the bottom.

Daunted by the expanse of stairs, he mounted the banister and slid down.

When he knelt and held her, she was laughing. Then, smiling, she closed her eyes and died.

It took him a long frozen moment to realize what had happened and to feel on his arms her broken body, too twisted to attempt revival.

She died in my arms, he thought. The bell rang, I fell out of bed, I called, she fell hard, I slid down the banister, she laughed, and she died in my arms. It's a story not to be told.

Ignoring his painful foot, he carried her up to her bed and straightened her out, weeping when bones cracked as he forced them back into place.

At last he rang for help and purposely fell to the floor to explain his injury. He told those who came that he had found Lady Anne like that and had fallen in his hurry to get to her. Later, he sent out word that she had died of unknown causes.

When all the rites were over, guests and family gone, children in their own rooms, he walked with a cane to Anne's study.

At her desk, he looked around at the boxes he knew were full of papers, more than twenty years of her work. He lifted a garden stone she used for a paper weight from a small stack of paper, and found this crossed-out note on the top sheet:

> Love, and all beauty,
> is seen
> not with the eye
> but with the mind

Aloud, he said, "Anne, love, you said about yourself, 'My meaning is in my pen.' I believe now that *my* meaning is in *your* pen."

He set to work.

1592: FINALE

At the intermission of the opening of the new play, *Romeo and Juliet*, Burghley left the group of courtiers around the queen to seek out Vere and Elizabeth, Oxford's second wife (Anne had been dead for four years).

Burghley, at age 62, was white-haired, straight, sharp-eyed, and with an assurance evidencing his status as the queen's most trusted advisor.

"A fine performance," he said.

"Indeed," replied Elizabeth, whose bejeweled green sleeves did not detract from her own glow. She was a woman who was always engaged, always attentive, always interested.

"It's a delight to see the play so well done after the many years since I first read it," said Burghley.

"You read it?" Asked Elizabeth.

Vere, now a little stout in his early forties, led his wife to a corner away from the crowd and beckoned Burghley to join them.

"Surely, Burghley, you do not wish this kind of conversation to be overheard," he said.

"Right, we have kept the secret for many years. I shall be careful. And aye, my lady, I read an early version, written by my daughter, Anne, after she read a similar story in Golding's translation of Ovid, and I am astonished to see Anne's work in performance.

"Lady Oxford, I must tell you that from the time Anne learned to use a pen she wrote, and she wrote, and she wrote. And when my little girl was not at her desk writing, she was reading.

"She was a gifted reader, Lady Oxford, very fast and retentive. Her mother tried to make her understand that, for a woman, writing is entirely worthless, and she prayed every day for Anne's deliverance from such nonsense.

"But Anne kept on writing, and I did not try to discourage her, for she was harming no one. She did not seem to me to be obsessed; she was always ready to interrupt her writing and chat.

"I think she wrote simply for her own pleasure and fulfillment, the way some women paint or embroider.

"And later, when she lived in my household while Vere lived on the continent, I would often ask to see her work and I would read it with a pleasure of my own.

"She wrote stories and poems and even then some plays, and I assumed they were all destroyed after she died. Clearly I was wrong. She began this *Romeo and Juliet* drama before she married. What I am seeing here tonight is much more fully developed and quite splendid.

"I have not gone to the theater in years. So, tell me, Vere, have other works of hers been adapted to be performed here?"

"Aye," Vere answered, "they have. I worked on some and gave them to a member of this company—to Will Shakespeare.

"Why? In God's name, why?"

"To preserve them. As a writer, a poet, myself, I found them too worthy to destroy, but at the same time I felt I must protect Anne's name—and mine, too—from the disgrace of such scandalous activity as writing plays.”

“You gave them to Shakespeare, did you? All of them? That was a great stack of paper.”

“My Lord,” said Elizabeth, “My husband has not yet given away everything your daughter wrote. Forgive me, Edward, for speaking of this. My Lord, it is not only your daughter’s writing that you see in this theater. Edward has been making her work into practical theater— plays. He is not yet finished with that great stack of paper. I am his copyist, you see.”

“She is more than my copyist, Burghley,” said Vere. “She keeps me busy with the plays. She keeps me happy in many ways,” he said smiling at his wife it great warmth.

“You are besotted, my son,” said Burghley.

“Nay,” he teased, “Who could care for such a monkey?”

“Another monkey,” Elizabeth answered.

Before this night, Burghley had not studied Elizabeth. What he now observed was a tall slender brunette in her mid-thirties with a transparent look of happiness with her life and comfort with herself.

“You, my son,” said Burghley, “are Lady Elizabeth’s life. You are to be envied.”

“I realize that Anne was much less dependent. Mayhap her scholarly bent and her creativity took an unwelcome precedence over . . . other things.”

“Despite this lack of full wifeliness, Vere, you saw value in Anne’s writing—value enough to preserve it.”

”Indeed, Burghley. However, I have made some changes in Anne’s manuscripts. Some needed very little change. Some were mere summaries that I have expanded. Some were complete, but—you knew her—she believed in happy endings, and happy endings are not always believable. And some of her dialogue and conversation seemed, well, too learned. Shakespeare also has rearranged a few scenes to make them easier to enact on stage.

"I regret that I did not see their value when she was alive." said Burghley. "I would have liked to give her more than my approval; I would have liked to give her true praise. I loved her dearly. You know, Lady Elizabeth, that I had her buried at Westminster Abbey in a grave marked with a small statue of myself and an inscription I wrote."

"Tell me what you wrote," said Elizabeth.

"It reads,

> His eyes dim with tears
> for the loss of those who were dear to him
> beyond the whole race of womankind.'

"So, Anne, Edward, and Will composed these works for the theater, eh? What I have seen I like very well. And Lady Elizabeth, I thank you for this intelligence. I am pleased beyond measure to know that Anne's spirit lives in these plays, even though no one knows it as hers.

"Anne, Edward, and Will— a splendid trio. Only one of that three will receive the credit, and we, another three, alone in all the world, know a great secret—that a splendid trio together could *shake* a pen to *spear* words into powerful life. Let us vow to keep swear to the secret."

They joined hands and said, one after the other. "I swear by the Almighty Trinity to keep the secret of who wrote the Shakespeare plays."

But Lady Elizabeth Oxford crossed her fingers behind her back. She thought,

> *I plan to leave enough hints and suggestions for future historians to discover the genius, William Shakespeare, to have been Edward DeVere, Lord Oxford, my husband. And I will assure that the entire credit goes to him. The man named Shakespeare is nothing but an almost illiterate actor and will certainly disappear in history. And as for the willful, self righteous, unwifely Lady Anne, she deserves no acclaim, and her scripts will just disappear.*

FINIS